D1481233

Perhaps I'll be an Orpple

Story by Z. Hackett
Illustrated by V. Snyker

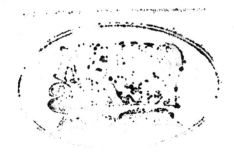

Perhaps I'll be an Orpple
The Orpple Project

YCG, LLC dba The Y.O.U. Institute

All rights reserved © 2016

ISBN: 978-1-889211-04-6

THE DISCOVERY SOURCE
Published and distributed by
The Discovery Source Inc.
PO Box 3350
Vista, CA 92085

www.thediscoverysource.com

The Orpple Project promotes Peace Education.
It is designed to educate children about human differences
and encourage tolerance, understanding and acceptance.
The message is in identifying natural talents
while supporting the potential
of one's self and others.

The Orpple Project includes:

Perhaps I'll be an Orpple **Storybooks**
for family and classroom
Teacher's Curriculum (preschool - first grade)
Supplementary activity materials
Songbook celebrating nature with lyrics
that can be sung to popular childood tunes, and a
Play where children can re-enact
the journey to uniqueness.

Dedication

To my son David, for inspiring this story during a
mother-son creative story time moment.
To my other children Jamie, Jonathan, Becca, and my
granddaughter, Sophie Rose.
Each continue to remind me every day to embrace
the differences each of us has to offer,
&
To my husband David, for honoring my sensitive nature
and helping me to make a great jam.

Once upon a time...

there was a traveling seed in search of fertile ground,

needing to plant itself before springtime came around.

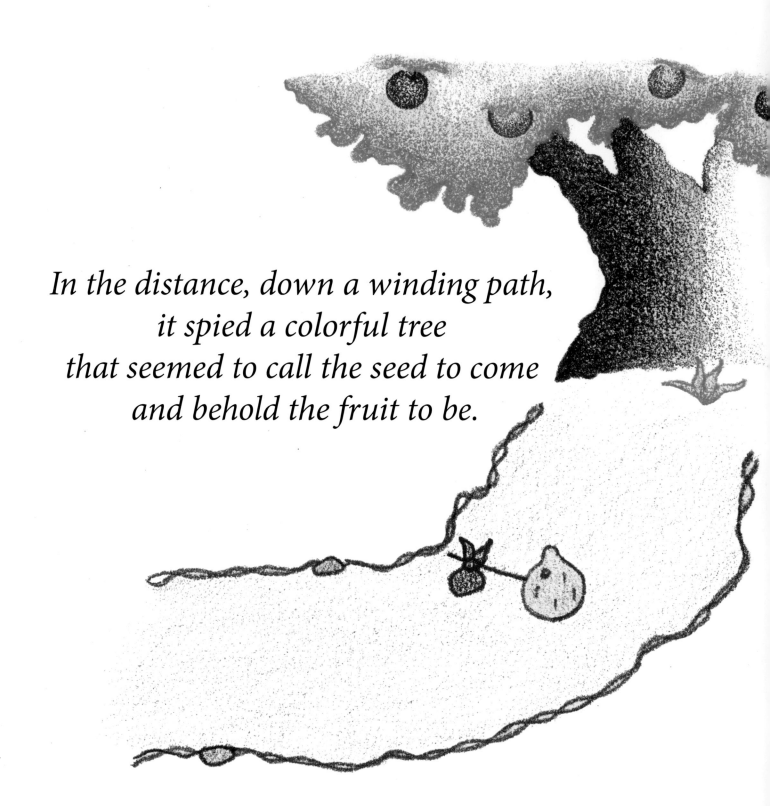

In the distance, down a winding path,
it spied a colorful tree
that seemed to call the seed to come
and behold the fruit to be.

The seed answered the request,
and swiftly rolled its way,
and when it reached the mighty trunk,
looked up as if to say,

"Is it true I see the apples
growing with the others?
Is it true I see the oranges
are your sisters and your brothers?

Why is it that
you both live
on the branches
of this tree?

How is it that
you get along
when you're
different as
can be?

The oranges,
they are soft
and juicy
and most
desirable to eat

and
the apples with
their bright
red skin,
are so shiny,
crisp and sweet.

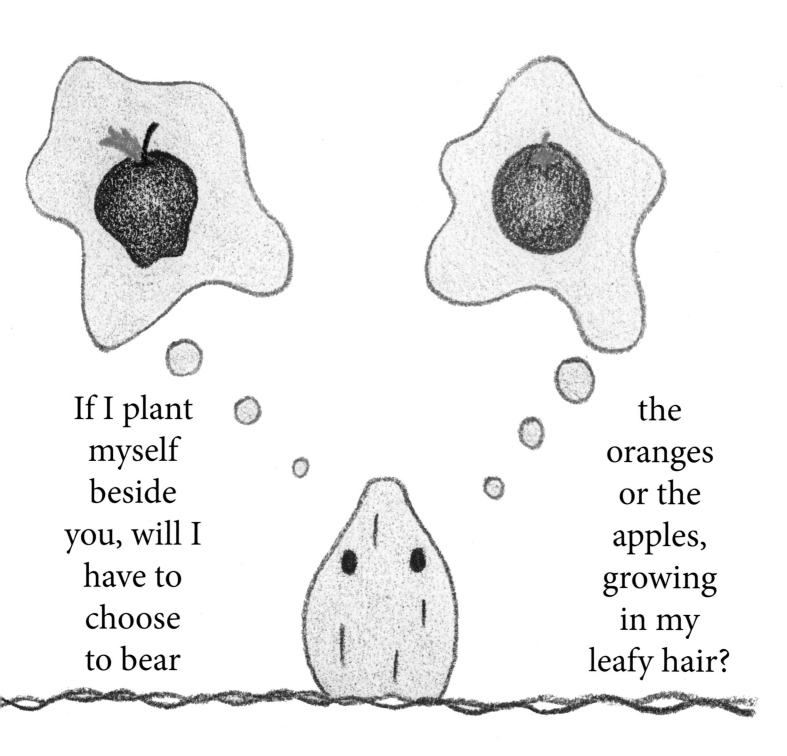

If I plant
myself
beside
you, will I
have to
choose
to bear

the
oranges
or the
apples,
growing
in my
leafy hair?

Perhaps I'll be a home
that chooses oranges for my fruit.

The bumpy skin when taken off,
leaves wedges that are cute.

They give you friendly nourishment
when you squeeze them for their drink

and boost your body's energy
when you need the strength to think.

But the apples have a lot to offer
and make a juice they call their own,
and if you mix them up just right,
it's a sauce that you'll take home.

Oh! I'm having trouble
trying to decide.
Should I bear the orange or apple?
Perhaps I ought to hide.

I'll hide for just a little while
until my thoughts are clear
on what it is I want to be
before springtime gets too near.

I'll snuggle in the softened ground
beneath my seedy feet
and cover up my little head
in case the birds should want to eat.

Hmmmm…this is warm and cozy.
I'm getting sleepy under here.
It's time to rest my little thoughts
and wait for a decision to come near."

The traveling seed fell deep asleep
beneath the earthly cover,
and its hidden body began to grow
next to the mighty other.

It tossed its dusty blanket
to sprout above the ground
and when the birds sang from its limbs,
it awoke to hear their sound.

22

"Oh my!" said the little tree.
"I'm not a traveling seed.
I grew a sturdy wooden base,
getting all the sleep I need.

I thought that it would give me strength
to decide which fruit to bear,
but now that I'm already a tree,
I guess I shouldn't care.

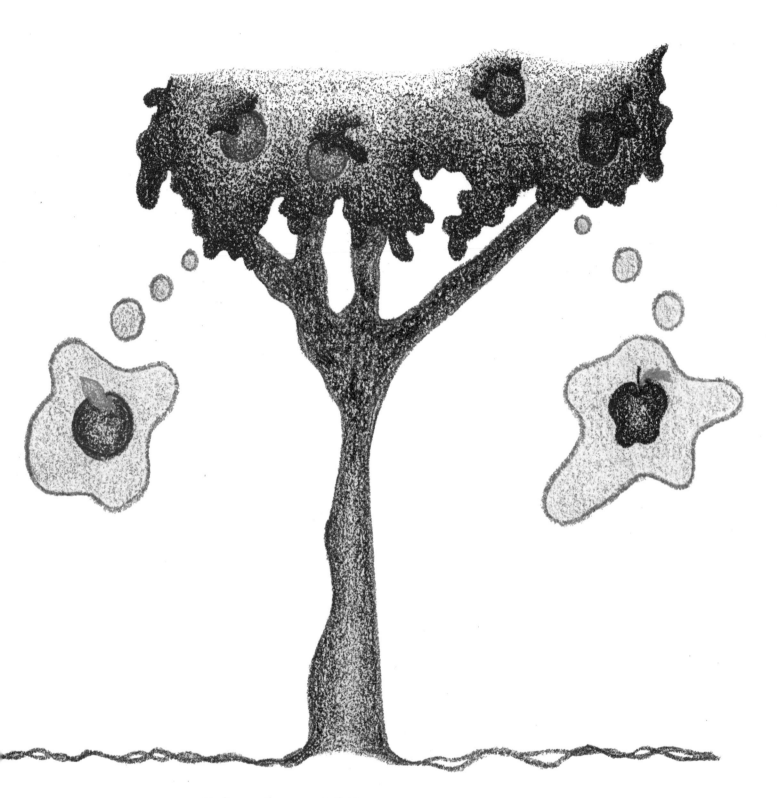

It's okay if I grow oranges.
I like the way they smell,
and if I'm home for apples,
I'm happy just as well.

25

Perhaps, I'll be an 'orpple'
and have the best of both their gifts,
with orpples falling to the ground
when the fragile branches shift.

They'll be juicy and quite shiny,
tasting sweet as golden honey

with little wedges that come apart
and insides that are speckled funny.

What's this I see
on my thickening branch?
A purple little sphere?
I think it's my own creation!
Oh, I think it's dear!

28

Look at its pretty shape,
and soft and satin skin!
I do not know its heavenly name,
but I know it's born within.

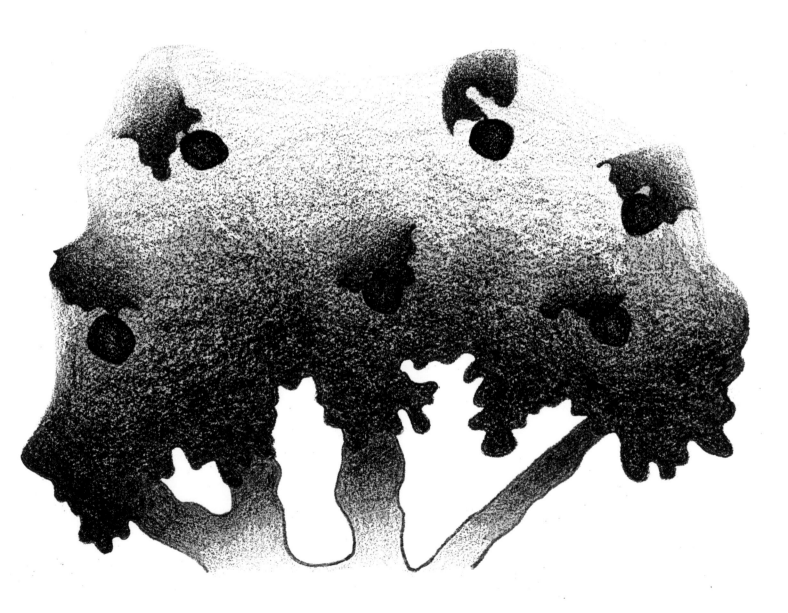

I know this thing of beauty
has a name that's bound to come.
What's that I hear? What's that you say?

To most it's called a 'plum?'

A plum! A plum! My fruit's a plum!
And I thought I'd have to choose.
I'm different from all the other fruit.

What a lovely piece of news!

I'm told that I am beautiful
and I make a wonderful jam,
and

I'm glad to be the gift
of who it is I am!"

The End

Perhaps I'll be an Orpple Song

Lyrics by J. Blink
Can be sung to the tune of *Bingo Was His Name-O*

There was a seed in search of fruit
It did not have a name-o
What shall I become?
What shall I become?
What shall I become?
It wondered night and day-o

It traveled far and found a tree
That grew oranges and apples
What shall I become?
What shall I become?
What shall I become?
An orange or an apple?

I could be juicy as an orange
  Or shiny like an apple
  What shall I become?
  What shall I become?
  What shall I become?
  Perhaps I'll be an orpple

The little seed then fell asleep
  And woke up as a plum tree
  What shall I become?
  What shall I become?
  What shall I become?
  Its heart was filled with glee

So, if you don't know who to be
  And wonder what to do
  What shall I become?
  What shall I become?
  What shall I become?
  Be happy you are you!